lunch

sniff
sniff

This book is for Rochelle

Special thanks to Laura for her patience and
to David and Indigo for their endurance

ISBN 0-590-46765-4

12 11 10 9 8 7 6 5 4 3   4 5 6 7 8/9

Printed in the U.S.A.   14

First Scholastic printing, September 1993

Designed by Denise Fleming

sniff

sniff

The illustrations were created in handmade paper.

lunch

Denise Fleming

SCHOLASTIC INC.

New York   Toronto   London   Auckland   Sydney

Mouse was *very* hungry.
He was so hungry,

he ate
a crisp
white —

turnip,

tasty

orange —

carrots,

sweet
yellow —

corn,

tender
green —

peas,

tart
blue —

berries,

sour
purple —

grapes,

shiny

red —

apples,

and juicy pink —

watermelon,

crunchy
black seeds
and all.

Then,

he took a nap
until . . .

yellow corn

green peas

blue berries

pink watermelon

white turnip

black seeds

orange carrots

purple grapes

red apples